Fragments of a Feeling

Fragments of a Feeling

A Philosophy of Love

Even the most fleeting love can shift the foundation of who we are...

Naman Goswami

AMARYLLIS

AMARYLLIS

An imprint of Manjul Publishing House Pvt. Ltd.
• C-16, Sector 3, Noida, Uttar Pradesh 201 301, India
Website: www.manjulindia.com

Registered Office:
• 2nd Floor, Usha Preet Complex, 42 Malviya Nagar,
Bhopal 462 003 – India

Distribution Centres
Ahmedabad, Bengaluru, Chennai, Hyderabad,
Kochi, Kolkata, Mumbai, Noida, Pune

Fragments of a Feeling: A Philosophy of Love by Naman Goswami

This paperback edition first published in India in 2026

ISBN 978-93-7317-727-4

Cover image: adobe stock.com

Printed and bound in India by Repro India Limited

If you find fragments of your own heart in these pages,
then maybe, in some quiet way, we have loved together.

Contents

Preface

Fragments of a Feeling: A Philosophy of Love

There are some experiences that don't fully leave us.

And sometimes, they return not as memories, but as questions.

This book began as a collection of questions I couldn't answer.

Not because they were complex, but because they were too human.

Why does love ache even when it's given freely?

Why do we attach, even knowing that everything is bound to change?

Is love truly permanent, or is it just a brief moment of grace we chase in different faces?

I did not write this book as a teacher, nor as someone who has healed.

I wrote it as someone who felt everything deeply and needed to make sense of it.

These chapters are not arguments or conclusions—they are meditations, scattered and stitched, like pages torn from a diary and held together with philosophy.

At times, I questioned if what I felt was even love.

Other times, it was too much to name it anything else.

And in that confusion, in that ache, I began to observe not just my pain, but the patterns, the silence, the natural rise and fall of emotion like tides. What you hold in your hands is not a story about someone else.

It's a mirror.

A slow unraveling of what it means to feel, to give, to suffer, and yet… to continue loving.

Not because it will be returned—but because that's what the soul does.

This is for the ones who gave more than they received.

For those who stayed longer in someone's heart than they were allowed to.

And for anyone who ever sat quietly and wondered:

"Was it love, or was it just me, loving alone?"

If you find fragments of your own heart in these pages, then maybe, in some quiet way, we have loved together.

Introduction

Between thought and feeling...

This is not a book you read.

It's a mirror you pass by.

You might see yourself. Or someone you lost. Or someone you were once becoming.

There are no heroes here. No answers.

Only fragments. Shards of thoughts left behind by feelings that refused to die quietly.

This book may not change your life.

But it might change the way you remember.

The way you look at someone from a distance.

The way silence feels when it's shared.

The way love sounds when it is no longer spoken.

Nothing in these pages asks for belief.

But if you read carefully, something inside you may begin to soften.

Something unnamed. Something untouched.

Something that was waiting for a language.
And maybe you'll walk away from this book
not with clarity, but with a deeper kind of confusion.
The kind that doesn't demand fixing.
Only awareness.

—*Fragments of a Feeling*

1

Why Do We Love?

"To love is not to possess, not to hold, not to desire, but to observe, without becoming anything."

Have we ever truly asked—*why do we love?*

Not as a romantic idea, not as an answer we want to hear, but as a serious inward question. We say we fall in love, we say we are in love, we even say we've lost love, but do we ever sit still with the question: *what is this thing we call love, and why do we need it so deeply?*

Most of the time, our love is a response. A movement. A reaction born out of loneliness, habit, or memory.

We want to be loved because it gives us a sense of being important in someone's world.

We want to hold someone close because it distracts us from the fact that we don't know how to be close to ourselves. So, is that love—or is it an escape?

Love, as we often live it, is full of expectation.

We want something back. We want security, we want attention, we want someone to make us feel whole. We do not say it aloud, but somewhere in our minds there is a quiet deal being made: "I will love you, if you do not leave me." Or worse—"I will love you, if you make me feel enough."

But love that demands is not love. It is fear.

Fear of abandonment, fear of emptiness, fear of being unseen.

When you look at a tree, and it simply exists—not for you, not against you—you don't want to own it. You don't ask it to give you something. You just watch it, and it moves something in you.

Can love be like that?

Can we love someone and let them be?

Can we hold someone without trying to change them, fix them, keep them?

Maybe we love, not because we are full, but because we are fragmented.

And in loving someone, we feel, if only for a moment, that the pieces are coming together. But that feeling fades, doesn't it? The person cannot carry our brokenness forever. The love becomes weight. The other becomes a mirror—and we blame them for showing us what we still haven't healed.

So again, we return to the question—*why do we love?*

Is it because we want to become someone in another's eyes?

Is it because we fear being no one at all?

Or is there a love that exists when there is no fear?

No past. No future. No desire to hold or to keep. Just love—present, simple, alive.

Such a love cannot be practiced. It cannot be forced.

It arises when the mind is quiet, when the heart is still, when we are not trying to become anything at all.

Perhaps we have never truly loved.

We have only tried to feel safe.

And maybe the beginning of real love is the ending of this need.

The Room Without a Door

He sat across from her, not saying anything.

Not because there was nothing to say,
but because there was nothing to protect.

No performance. No masks. No waiting for the perfect moment.

She looked at him once, and then looked away.

He didn't ask why. He didn't need her eyes to feel close.

For the first time, he wasn't trying to be loved.

He wasn't afraid she would leave.

He wasn't counting the seconds of silence.

He just let her exist.

And in that quiet room,
something like love floated between them—
a love with no name,
no future,
no fear.

2

The Kinds of Love

"Maybe love hurts so much because we never really understood what love is."

When we speak of love, we often speak of only one kind, the romantic kind.

We believe that love means attraction, passion, wanting to be close to someone.

And when that kind of love fades or fails, we think love itself has betrayed us.

But the truth is, there is not just one kind of love.

There are many.

There are loves that begin like accidents—unexpected, beautiful, and painful.

You don't plan them. They just happen when life opens a small crack, and someone slips through.

There are loves that make you *feel seen* for the first time, and because of that, you mistake them for forever.

There are quiet loves, the kind that never get spoken about.

No confessions, no closure, just a few moments that keep replaying in your head for years.

Sometimes, the most powerful love is the one that never found words.

There are selfish loves too—the ones where you only want to be loved back, not love.

You hold someone, not because you care, but because you can't stand being alone.

And then there's the kind that matures silently.

No drama, no fireworks, just presence.

You don't need to say much. You don't even need to meet often.

You just know the bond doesn't depend on time or distance anymore.

There are loves that save you and loves that destroy you.

And sometimes, they're the same one.

The person who teaches you how to feel also teaches you what loss means.

That's how love works—it gives and it takes, equally.

Then there's the rarest kind—the one that stays even after everything ends.

When you no longer need the person to exist to still feel love.

It's not longing, not obsession.

It's peace.

You just carry them softly, like light; no bitterness, no wish to return.

Maybe these are not types of love at all.

Maybe they're the different *ages* of love inside you.

Each one leaving a trace, shaping how you understand the next.

Love doesn't become wiser with time.

It just grows quiet. It sheds the noise, the need to be understood, the urge to be returned.

After a while, you stop looking for it in faces and names.

You start noticing it in small things—the way sunlight touches a wall, the way silence holds you when words fail.

And somehow, love is still there, steady and unseen, even when everything else has gone.

3

Is Love Permanent, or Just a Momentary Truth?

"What if forever was just a feeling we had in a moment that ended?"

I have often asked myself this, and I ask you now—is love meant to last, or is it meant to change us and leave?

Why does it begin with such intensity, with such certainty, only to dissolve like mist in morning light? Was that intensity false, or was it the only truth that ever existed?

They say love is eternal, but people aren't. People leave. They fall out of love. They forget. They change. And yet, even after their footsteps have vanished from our lives, the love remains somewhere like a scent trapped in old pages, like an echo in a room long emptied.

If love was real, how could it end?

And if it ended, was it ever real?

We often confuse presence with permanence. Just because she was there when I needed her most, just because she looked at me once like I was the only person in the world—I believed she would stay. I believed that moment stretched into forever. But what I loved was not her body alone; it was the world that lit up around her—the way my soul responded when she entered the room.

Can such a thing truly vanish?

I've started to feel that what we usually call "love" is often just the fear of being alone, the hunger for meaning, the hope that someone else can complete what we couldn't finish inside ourselves.

And maybe that's why it fails. Because it begins as an escape, not an overflowing.

True love, if it exists, is not a transaction. It doesn't say, *"I give you this, so stay."*

It doesn't ask for forever. It is its own reward.

Most people don't fall in love with someone.

They fall in love with how someone makes them feel.

And feelings, like weather, are destined to change.

Maybe love isn't meant to last in form. Maybe it only lasts in transformation—in the way it cracks you open, rearranges your soul, and teaches you to see beauty where you once saw absence.

Maybe the question isn't *"Is love permanent?"*

Maybe it is: *"Can I remain loving, even after the object of love is gone?"*

Some say love is just a biological accident—chemicals designed to trick us into bonding, breeding, continuing the species. But if that were true, why do people mourn a heartbreak as if mourning a death? Why do some stay faithful to a ghost of love that hasn't touched them in years?

Nature may want survival, but the soul wants something else—something not found in logic or function. The soul wants connection. The soul wants to lose itself.

So maybe love isn't natural. Maybe it's supernatural.

Maybe that's why it hurts.

Because it doesn't belong to this world entirely.

And perhaps that's why we write—not to hold on, but to remember what it felt like when our soul briefly touched something infinite. Even if it didn't stay.

I remember the first time I saw her. She wasn't looking at me, just walking with a friend, orange bag swaying, keychains clinking softly like wind chimes in a lazy afternoon breeze.

Nothing dramatic happened. But I remember the feeling. Like the world paused—not because she saw me, but because I saw something in her that I didn't yet understand.

Maybe that was love. Or maybe it was just the start of a question that still hasn't found its answer.

The Teacup on Her Balcony

He used to bring her tea every morning. Not because she asked, but because he loved the quiet way she held the cup—both hands wrapped around it, as if it held the warmth of the world.

They never said "forever." They didn't need to. For three years, that morning ritual was their religion.

One winter, she left. No anger, no cruelty. Just silence. Something had changed—perhaps in her, perhaps in the rhythm of life.

He still made two cups every morning. He still placed one on the balcony rail where she used to stand.

After some time, he stopped. Not because he didn't love her anymore, but because something inside him had accepted:

Some love is real.

And yet, not all love is meant to last.

Some love is like the steam rising from a cup of tea
warm, beautiful, true
but fading, all the same.

4

Do We Love the Person, or Just Our Own Feeling?

"She left long ago, but the feeling stayed, so was it ever her I loved, or just the way I felt in her light?"

I remember the curve of her name more than the voice that spoke it.

I remember how she smiled once, maybe twice, but I've repeated that memory a hundred times.

And every time it grows softer, warmer, almost unreal.

I wonder…

Was I in love with her?

Or was I simply in love with what awakened inside me when she was near?

There is a quiet deception hidden inside love—a sweet one, but a deception nonetheless. We think we are choosing a person. But sometimes, we are only choosing a version of ourselves that feels whole in their presence. And when they go, it's not just them we lose, it's that version of ourselves we can no longer become.

So, I ask:

Was she the destination, or merely the mirror?

Sometimes I think she was just the trigger.

A matchstick. A window.

The thing that helped me access something that was already inside me—a capacity to feel, to long, to soften, to surrender.

But in that moment, I didn't see it as self-awakening.

I saw it as *her*.

There is a cruelty in this realization.

That maybe she wasn't the feeling—she was just the cause of it.

You see, if I close my eyes and imagine that someone else had smiled that same way, said those same words, looked at me with that same quiet understanding… would I have fallen just as hard?

Would it still have been called love?

We are taught to believe that love is about the other.

But what if love is just an internal explosion, and the other person is merely the spark?

And what if… that's why people fall out of love?

Not because the other has changed—but because the feeling has changed. The mirror cracks, and we no longer like the version of ourselves we see reflected back.

I think most of us fall for the intoxication, the thrill, the hunger, the sweetness of not being alone. And when the intoxication fades, we call it heartbreak. But maybe, what truly fades is the illusion, and what remains, if anything, is love.

When I think of her now, I no longer ask why she left. I no longer ask if she still thinks of me. I ask, *did I ever truly love her, or just what she lit up inside me for a while?*

Because if it was real love, it wouldn't need possession.

It would have accepted the goodbye.

Maybe love, in its purest form, isn't about needing someone to stay.

It's about wishing them well, even if they never return.

Maybe that's what it means to truly love—

to still bow your head in gratitude for the mirror they once held up to you.

To bless the space where they once stood.

To let them go… without wishing they'd come back.

We say we loved them.

But often, we only loved the way they made us forget we were alone.

A boy walks the same route every evening just to pass by the same bookstore window.

Inside, a girl sits behind the counter, reading.

They never speak.

She never looks up.

One day, she isn't there.

He stops walking that route.

And never forgets her.

The Mirror in Her Words

He loved the way she laughed at his jokes, the way her eyes sparkled when she spoke about books, and how she listened—really listened.

But one day, she stopped laughing. Her eyes were tired. She no longer reacted with warmth, only silence.

And slowly, he felt his love fading.

That's when he wondered—

Was it *her* he loved?

Or the version of himself he saw reflected in her gaze?

The joy she gave him, the meaning he felt in her presence, the way *he* felt when *she* was around.

Maybe he hadn't fallen in love with her.

Maybe he had fallen in love with the way she made him feel.

5

Is Love a Natural Force or Just Nature's Sweetest Trick?

What if love was never meant to be eternal?

What if nature, in its quiet brilliance, designed it only as a trick

a spark to make two souls collide, just long enough to create life,

before they drift apart like seeds from the same fruit?

We grow up believing in soulmates, in forever, in a person who fits our breath like a second skin.

But nature doesn't care for forever. It only cares for continuation.

Love, then, might be nothing more than a perfume released by the body, a song the blood hums to draw another body closer.

What we call *destiny* might just be a chemical alignment.

What we name *divine* may be deeply, quietly biological.

It's a hard truth to swallow.

That the poetry we write about love could be carved not by God,

but by evolution.

And yet… there's something within us that still *believes.*

Still hopes.

Still aches not just to be touched, but to be understood.

Not just to mate, but to merge.

And that longing, that aching… doesn't feel like survival.

It feels like something older, quieter, holier.

Perhaps love is both:

A lie told by nature, and a truth whispered by the soul.

Maybe it begins as biology—desire, instinct, proximity.

But it becomes something else

the moment we sit in silence with someone,

and see in their eyes a loneliness that looks like our own.

It becomes something else

when we hold their sadness without trying to fix it.

When we stay even when we no longer feel the high.

When we choose presence over pleasure.

That is not nature's trick.

That is *will.*

That is *consciousness.* That is the part of us untouched by evolution, the part that dares to love not because we must, but because we want to.

So, no—maybe love is not natural.

Because nature doesn't care about staying.

Nature doesn't care about holding a dying hand or loving someone through madness.

Nature doesn't care about letters written to someone who no longer writes back.

But you did.

You still do.

And that, in itself, is a rebellion.

Love is not natural.

It is human.

It is the most unnecessary, irrational, divine thing we do to look at another person and say,

"I choose you, even though I don't have to."

The Algorithm of the Heart

Kashish and Yash didn't meet under falling stars or in the quiet corner of a bookstore.

They met in the endless scroll of a dating app, two faces caught in the glow of each other's screens.

At first, it felt like choice. She liked his playlist filled with songs that sounded like summer evenings; he loved the way her texts felt like they were written with a smile. They both swiped right, thinking they had found each other by chance.

But Yash once read that these apps didn't just match people, they studied them. They learned the hour loneliness knocked on your door, the type of eyes that made you pause, the laugh that made you linger.

Months passed. Their love bloomed in voice notes, coffee dates, and shared sunsets. And yet, one night, Kashish whispered, "Do you think we met because we were meant to… or because something out there knew we'd click?"

Yash smiled in the dark, but inside he wondered. Was their love the poetry of the universe, or just a beautiful trick, nature, technology, and biology conspiring to keep two hearts beating in sync?

And if it was a trick, he thought, it was the sweetest one he'd ever fall for.

6

Love or Attachment—Are They the Same?

Sometimes, the hand you're holding feels like home.

But is it love?

Or is it just the relief of not being alone?

We rarely pause to ask.

Because both love and attachment can feel the same in the beginning:

a rush, a softness, a sense of belonging.

But the difference emerges in silence, in stillness—when nothing is happening, and yet something within us still aches.

People often confuse love with attachment, but the two are not the same. We can get attached to a coffee mug, a childhood sweater, or the corner of a room where the sunlight falls just right—things that can never love us back. Attachment can exist without love, but love without attachment is rare, and perhaps that's why we hold on to people the way we hold on to objects, afraid not of losing them, but of losing the comfort they give us.

Attachment says, "Don't leave me; I can't breathe without you."

Love says, "I want you to be free, even if that freedom takes you away from me."

Attachment clings.

Love lets go, and still stays in spirit.

Attachment is born of fear—fear of loss, fear of pain, fear of emptiness.

Love, in its purest form, is fearless.

It does not demand.

It does not shrink or expand based on attention.

It simply is, like sunlight on skin, not asking to be touched, only to be felt.

There was a time I thought I loved her.

Now I wonder if I just needed her presence to fill a silence I was too scared to sit with.

Did I love her voice, or just the way it covered the noise in my own mind?

Did I love her touch, or just the way it reminded me I existed?

We often confuse love with need.

But love does not need.

It gives, and gives, and gives—not out of poverty, but abundance.

Attachment fears change.

Love dances with it.

Attachment tries to freeze a moment and hold it forever.

Love understands that even the most beautiful flowers must be allowed to wilt.

So many of us are just trying to heal something.

We look for bandages in other people, medicine in a kiss, home in a body.

And when they pull away, we say, "They abandoned me," but perhaps what hurts is not their leaving.

It is the wound we never healed—the one that existed long before they came.

If you are aching, ask yourself:

Am I hurting because I lost love—

or because I lost a story I was telling myself through someone else?

True love does not enslave you to a person.

It liberates you from the need to possess them.

True love doesn't complete you.

It reminds you that you were whole long before anyone arrived.

Maybe love and attachment aren't opposites; maybe they are twins, born in the same moment, but destined to walk different paths.

And maybe part of growing up or growing in is learning to recognize which one we are truly feeling.

And having the courage to let go of the one that chains us, even if it calls itself love.

The Umbrella in the Rain

They used to walk home together, sharing one umbrella.

He would always tilt it slightly more towards her side, getting half-wet himself, but smiling like it was the most natural thing in the world.

One day, she didn't come.

The rain still fell.

He stood there, holding the umbrella, alone.

He waited, not just for her, but for the feeling she gave.

He missed her presence, her words, her warmth.

But more than anything, he missed not feeling alone.

And so, he asked himself:

Was this love?

Or just the fear of losing comfort?

Was it her he missed, or the shelter she became?

7

Is It Possible to Love Without Attachment?

"Real love isn't about keeping someone, it's about vibing with their soul, even if they drift out of your playlist someday."

We often confuse love with attachment. We believe that to love someone deeply, we must hold them close, bind them to us, and make their presence certain. But attachment is not the same as love—it is the fear of losing love.

To love without attachment is to give without needing. It is not the absence of feeling, but the absence of possession. True love flows freely—it does not bind, it does not bargain, it does not demand proof. Attachment says, *"I need you, therefore I love you."* Love says, *"I love you, therefore I wish you well—whether you are with me or not."*

When we are complete within ourselves, love becomes an offering rather than a transaction. It is no longer a need to be met, but a choice to be shared. We are no longer shaken by someone's distance or absence; our affection is steady, not because they never leave, but because our happiness is not chained to their presence.

This is not coldness—it is warmth without ownership, a closeness that doesn't cage. In this space, love is at its purest: a free, living thing that grows not by holding tighter, but by letting be.

In such love, your joy comes from seeing the other happy, even if their happiness unfolds in a world where you are no longer the centre. You continue to bless them in silence, not out of sacrifice, but because your love was never dependent on being chosen back.

And perhaps this is the highest love—one that cannot truly break, because there is nothing to break. It is unshaken by distance, untouched by rejection, and undefeated by time. It is a love that exists for its own sake, needing no reason, no reward, and no return.

"The purest love is the one that remains free to leave, yet chooses to stay."

"The Chat Bubble That Never Turned Blue"

There was this guy who met a girl in an online community. They started talking—not every day, not with any labels, just random conversations at 2 a.m. about music, movies, and things they couldn't tell anyone else.

He never asked her to call him every night. She never demanded constant updates. There were no "good morning" texts waiting like an obligation, only the surprise of a notification when it happened.

Months passed. They never met in person. But every conversation felt like finding a song you didn't know you needed. He never told her, "Don't talk to others," because he wasn't scared to lose her. She wasn't his to lose.

And then, one day, life took over. The chats became fewer, and eventually, the typing bubble stopped appearing. But instead of pain, he felt a quiet gratitude, because he realized he had loved someone without ever trying to own them. And that's why the ending didn't hurt.

8

The First Lie of Love

They say love is pure.

Unbiased. Deep. Soulful.

But is that how it begins?

Think back to your first school crush.

Was it about their values, their kindness, the way they held your silence?

Or was it about their face, their walk, the way everyone else looked at them?

Let's be honest—our first idea of love was shaped by faces, not feelings.

You saw it too.

In classrooms, on playgrounds, in corridors.

The tall boy with sharp features always had someone waiting for him.

The fair girl with the perfect hair always had secret admirers.

And the ones with softness in their voice, poetry in their minds, sincerity in their hearts?

They waited. They watched. They were passed by.

So how can we say love is pure,

when the person we choose often meets a standard, of looks, of charm, of social approval?

We don't fall in love with *just* a soul.

We fall in love with how someone fits the image we've built in our mind—often borrowed from films, reels, fairy tales, filtered photos.

We call it chemistry. But maybe it's *conditioning*.

We call it connection. But maybe it's *confirmation*, of the standard we think we deserve.

And this doesn't make us evil.

It just makes us honest. Human.

But we must ask:

If love begins from appearance,

if it chooses based on face, skin, height, posture

then where is the purity?

Is it love,

or just selection?

Eyes Lied First

It often starts with a glance.

The curve of a smile, the way someone walks, or how their hair falls over their face.

We don't fall in love with the soul at first. How could we?

We've only just seen their skin.

So, we begin with the surface—the face, the voice, the warmth of presence. We call it love, but maybe it's not. Maybe it's attraction dressed as forever.

We imagine a future. We build expectations on foundations we don't yet understand.

And here lies the first lie:

That the feeling which starts in the body will grow into something permanent in the heart.

Sometimes it does.

But most often, it doesn't.

Because beauty fades, and once the magic of newness wears off, only truth remains.

And if there's no truth beneath the attraction, everything begins to fall apart.

Yet we lie again, and again.

Because it's a beautiful lie.

It makes loneliness disappear, even if only for a while.

9

The Giver Always Walks Freer

The one who gave love walks ahead with peace; the one who only received carries the pain of absence.

It is often assumed that the one who gives more, who texts first, plans everything, makes the effort, must suffer the most when love ends.

But that's not true.

Because their love wasn't built on what they were receiving.

They gave not to bind, not to control, but because they felt something real inside.

They were complete in their act of giving.

They left no part of their emotion hidden.

And when it ends, they don't carry the burden of regret.

But the one who received, the one who got used to being checked on, loved, understood, seen.

They feel the cut much deeper.

Because now, something is missing.

Not just the person

But the *things* they brought with them:

The emotional support.

The comfort of being understood without asking.

The late-night calls.

The physical closeness.

The softness of being someone's priority.

This is why most people hurt so deeply in breakups.

Because they stop receiving what had become a daily emotional rhythm.

It's not always the person they miss; it's the version of themselves they were allowed to be in their presence.

Held. Heard. Loved. Desired.

And now, they are left with silence.

Silence that echoes.

Silence that feels like punishment.

"Moving on"—people say it like it's a clean decision.

But hearts do not move in straight lines.

They spiral.

They return.

They linger in the smell of a shirt, in the silence between songs, in the way your name still lives in my throat like a half-spoken prayer.

But what does it mean—to *move on*?

To forget?

To stop loving?

To feel nothing?

No, moving on is not the death of love.

It is the birth of understanding.

If you were the giver in the bond, if you poured your time, your care, your words, your patience, your little sacred routines, then your grief is quiet.

It holds no debt.

You gave what you had, without needing a return.

And that giving is freedom.

The giver suffers, yes.

But their suffering is clean.

There is no guilt in giving.

No emptiness in offering yourself fully.

But the one who only *received*—

who only took,

who depended on your presence like borrowed light—

they feel the collapse harder.

Because now, there is no one to fill their hollow.

No echo to answer them.

They are left not with grief, but with a craving.

And craving is more painful than heartbreak.

Because heartbreak ends.

Craving keeps wanting.

So yes, you can move on.

But only when you know what you *were* in the bond.

If you were love itself, not the one begging for it,

then you're already free.

Because love does not bind itself to outcome.

It is complete in its expression.

You loved. You gave. You stayed true.

That is your closure.

No grand ending. No apology needed.

Just the quiet knowledge:

I loved without needing to possess.

To move on is not to erase someone.
It is to remember them without resistance.
To let them exist in your memory like a soft river—
flowing, but no longer pulling you under.
That is not forgetting.
That is freedom.

"The Coffee That Was Never Paid For"

Every Friday, she would wait outside the college café, and I would show up with her usual: extra foam, no sugar, a dash of cinnamon. She never asked. I never told her why I did it.

At first, it felt like a habit. Then, it became something else.

It wasn't about the coffee.

It was about the small joy of giving, of seeing her eyes light up in that soft, unguarded way.

One day, she stopped coming. No texts. No explanation. The café line felt longer than usual. My hands didn't carry coffee that day, or the next.

But here's the strange part: there was no ache.

Because I had never been keeping score.

I hadn't been giving to get anything back, not love, not attention, not even a thank you.

When you're the giver, your happiness isn't chained to their presence.

You're free—because what you gave was never meant to be returned.

10

If It's Nature, It Must Change

"We say love is natural,
but forget that nature never stays the same."

We ask this often:

"Will you love me forever?"

And often we answer with hope, not truth.

But if love is a natural phenomenon—as we so often claim—then we must accept nature's nature:

It flows. It changes. It dies.

And then, astonishingly, it begins again.

No sunrise has ever lasted forever.

No storm has remained untouched by stillness.

No flower has refused to wilt.

No season has clung to permanence.

If love is born of nature,
then it must carry nature's rhythm
its cycle of birth, bloom, decay, and rebirth.

So perhaps the question isn't whether love is permanent or temporary.

Perhaps the real question is:

Can we love even when it begins to change form?

The pain comes not because love ends,

but because we expected it to remain unchanged.

We loved the *constancy*, not the *truth*.

We held on to *form*, not the *feeling*.

But love, like rivers, like stars, like our own breath, was never meant to be frozen.

Love that does not change was never alive to begin with.

Does that mean love fades?

Not necessarily.

Some love matures. It softens. It becomes quieter like rain that turns to mist.

Some love erupts again and again, like tides.

Some die completely, not because they were false, but because they were complete.

And some, rare and strange, become like light

not bound to time or face,

but illuminating whoever stands in its path.

So is love permanent or temporary?

It is neither.

It is alive.

And anything alive must be allowed to move, to grow, to die and to return in some other form.

If you try to imprison it in permanence, it will suffocate.

If you fear its impermanence, you will never fully live it.

To love truly is to say:

"If this ends tomorrow, I will still be grateful.

And if it stays forever, I will remain humble."

That is the only love worth calling real.

"The River She Loved"

She used to sit by the river every evening.

He would join her sometimes, and they'd speak of forever.

She once said, "This river is like you—calm, deep, always there."

But seasons came. The river swelled, flooded, turned wild.

Some days, it dried into a mere stream.

It never stayed the same.

And neither did he.

He no longer laughed at the same jokes. His silences grew longer, not softer. He wasn't cruel—just changed.

And she couldn't understand why.

But how could he remain the same?

Wasn't he, too, like the river?

11

When the Wall Doesn't Speak Back

"Even if you love without expectation, even if your heart is a temple, if all your prayers are answered with silence, the silence will begin to hurt."

They say real love means loving without asking anything in return.

That love is pure only when it expects nothing, no reply, no promise, no hand reaching back.

And maybe that's true.

But even the one who gives endlessly is still human.

Even the selfless heart longs, sometimes, for just a whisper that it mattered.

If you speak every day to a wall
not expecting it to move, not asking it to change
but just needing to release what lives inside you...
one day, the silence will feel heavy.

Not because you were selfish.

Not because your love wasn't pure.

But because you are not made of stone.

You can love like the ocean, endlessly,

but even the ocean aches for the pull of the moon.

So yes, you can love someone without needing them to love you back.

You can pour everything into that love, freely, like sunlight.

But even the sun grows tired when there is no sky to reflect its warmth.

You are allowed to feel empty.

You are allowed to feel the weight of giving.

You are allowed to say,

“I didn’t ask for anything, but I did hope.

And that hope became heavy.”

This is not weakness.

It is not failure.

It is the most human ache there is:

to give everything and still feel invisible.

Even saints cried.

Even gods longed to be seen.

What do we do?

We love.

And we also rest.

We give.

But we also remember:

“we are not born only to be givers.”

We deserve love that is not begged for.

That arrives not because we asked,

but because it *wanted* to.

And until then—

we love gently.

We give without killing ourselves.
Because love is not about becoming a martyr.
It's about becoming light, but not burning out.

Unread, But Not Unsent

There was a boy who fell in love with her voice before he even held her hand.

Not just the way she spoke but what she said, how she said it, and even what she left unsaid.

She replied to him once with a poem,

another time with a single emoji that made him smile for hours.

Even silence from her felt like music in the beginning because it still belonged to *her*.

He began to send her things.

Late-night thoughts, songs that reminded him of her, long paragraphs about sunsets and overthinking.

He wasn't asking for answers not always.

He just wanted to be heard.

But slowly, her replies became fewer.

Short. Dry. Mechanical.

One word. Then none.

He tried harder.

He said things more beautifully, more vulnerably—like someone tapping on glass, hoping someone is still inside.

But the messages were no longer reaching her.

They were bouncing back, silently.

That's when he realized… he wasn't in a conversation anymore.

He was standing in front of a wall.

And the wall doesn't speak back.
Still, some nights, he whispered to it.
Because what hurts more than silence
is the fear that no one is listening
and the memory of when someone did.

"We don't hold on to people; we hold on to the moments they made us feel alive."

12

Why Do We Hold On When It's Over?

"The heart does not follow time.
It holds on, not because it is foolish
but because it once felt something real,
and real things don't disappear quietly."

We often think the hardest part of love is the goodbye.

But it's not.

The hardest part is what comes after
when the person is gone,
but their presence still lives in everything around you.

The way you still check your phone.

The way certain songs still know where to hurt.

The way a scent, a street, or a sentence can undo you without warning.

You know it's over.

But your heart doesn't work like a switch.

It wasn't built for sudden endings.

It was built to stay—

even when staying becomes lonely.

So why do we hold on?

Because somewhere in us,

we believe that what was *felt* must still exist somewhere

if not in them,

at least in the echo.

Because memory is not a thing we choose.

It is a thing that *chooses* us.

Because even pain is sometimes easier than emptiness.

Because letting go feels like betrayal

not of the person,

but of the version of us that once believed in forever.

Holding on is not always about hope.

Sometimes, it is about grief.

Not grieving a person, but grieving the part of you that only existed with them.

The version of you that laughed like that.

That dreamed like that.

That felt safe in their eyes.

And maybe that's why letting go hurts:

Because we are not just losing *someone else*

we are also losing *ourselves.*

But here's a quiet truth:

Letting go does not mean forgetting.

It means choosing peace over punishment.

It means accepting that even the most beautiful rain eventually dries from the skin.

But that doesn't mean it didn't fall.

It means understanding:

"I loved, and I still carry it

but I will not keep bleeding where no healing arrives."

You're not weak for holding on.

You're just human.

And slowly, softly,

you'll realize that you don't have to forget love to move forward.

You only have to stop kneeling at its grave.

Because love was real, but so is your future.

13

To Witness Love Is a Rare Thing

"Not everyone is given the chance to love.
Fewer still get to be changed by it.
And even fewer are brave enough to feel it fully."

Some things in life are not meant to be possessed.

They are meant to be witnessed

to be held softly in the palms for a while,

before being returned to the wind.

Love is like that.

A phenomenon so rare, so inexplicably human,

that its mere presence should make us kneel in awe—not with fear, but with wonder.

So often we rush.

We want to name it, define it, hold it tightly before it slips.

But maybe love, at its purest, is not a thing to own.

It is a process,

a movement of energy through the soul,

unfolding like a flower in slow motion.
Not every love must become a story.
Some are just moments,
beautiful, painful, alive.
Pause for a moment.
Look at what you've been through.
The nights you stayed awake with a heart full of someone else.
The poems you never shared.
The longing you buried in silence.
The joy, the ache, the fear, the surrender.
You lived it.
You were awake in love.
And that is no small thing.
The world is full of people who never feel deeply.
Who move through relationships like checklists.
Who touch bodies but not souls.
But you—
you *loved.*
You listened to the trembling of your chest
and gave it space to speak.
You let someone matter to you.
Even if it ended.
Even if it hurt.
That's courage.
That's aliveness.
That's the rarest thing.
So instead of mourning that it didn't last,
what if you simply said:
"I was lucky to have seen it.
I was blessed to feel this strange, soft thunder in my chest.

I was part of something beautiful,
even if only for a moment."
Observe it like a sunrise.
You do not hold the sun.
You do not demand it stays.
But you watch it, breathless,
because you know:
this is rare.
And that is enough.
"Love is not rare; the eyes that can see it are."

14

The Heart's Capacity

Even after the flame dies, something still smolders. Not longing, not memory but the silent courage to love again.

When love ends, it does not always die—it mutates.

Sometimes into memory.

Sometimes into fear.

Sometimes... into silence.

The mind, a compulsive recorder, replays everything—the laughter, the betrayal, the promises.

And the heart, more honest than the brain, trembles: *Can I ever love again?*

Philosophers ask: *What is the self that loves?*

Is it merely memory—a conditioned pattern seeking warmth?

Or is there something deeper, something unnameable, that continues to seek union?

Osho would say: love is not a relationship, it is a state of being.

So if you have truly *become* love, then it is never over.

The person may change, the form may change—but the flowering remains.

And flowering, by its very nature, seeks the sun again.

So when love turns into hate, which it often does after breakups, we must ask: *Was it love or possession?*

Because real love does not become hatred.

Real love, when left behind, simply becomes compassion.

But still, the question remains—can we love again?

The answer lies not in effort, but in *awareness.*

To observe the pain, to not run from it.

To let it burn through you without turning to bitterness.

Ramana Maharshi spoke of the "I" that watches even heartbreak without attachment.

That witness is untouched.

And only from that stillness can another love rise—not as a replacement, but as a continuation of your inner expansion.

Loving again is not a betrayal of the past.

It is a sign that you have not closed your heart to life.

To love again is not weakness.

It is the most courageous act of a soul that refuses to give up its light.

Not everyone can do it.

But the one who becomes a giver, who no longer seeks to own, only to offer, is never afraid to love again.

Because for them, the source of love is not outside.

It is within.

We think we are free to love again, but often, we are only revisiting what hurt us, reshaping it in new faces, waiting for it to end differently. Memory, when held tightly, becomes a filter; it distorts the now, mistrusts joy, and guards against surrender.

But love demands surrender. It demands the risk of being shattered again, without the shield of what came before.

True love can only happen when the mind is still, when the past is not the measuring stick, and the self is not protecting itself from feeling. If you carry memory like armor, love will always bruise you. But if you drop it like an old skin, perhaps then love will touch you where even memory couldn't reach.

One does not need to forget to be free...

One only needs to stop *identifying* with what was.

"In love, endings are illusions. Only forms change. The essence remains, waiting to be lived again."

15

Fragments Without Response

What if the person you love never says it back?

What if they never call you by the name you whisper for them in your mind? What if you keep writing pages and they never even know a single word was about them? What if they never look at you the way you've looked at them a hundred times?

Is that still love?

We often think that love needs to be returned to become real. That unless the other person confirms it, touches it, names it, receives it, it doesn't count. But why do we believe that?

Is love only valid if it's mutual? Or can it exist alone—soft, unspoken, unresolved?

Most of us spend years in confusion, asking the same quiet question: *Do they love me too?*

And behind that, a deeper one: *Should they love me back for my love to matter?*

This is the ache no one talks about. When you feel everything—but don't know if the other person feels anything at all. When you wait for signs. When you replay words. When you read between silences and try to find answers in half-smiles.

You start building a relationship in your mind. You collect fragments, moments, eye contact, shared jokes, and try to shape them into something whole.

But what if they never respond?

What if they never even knew?

Does that make your love foolish, or does it make it pure?

We rarely talk about the dignity of unreturned love. The quiet strength it takes to love someone without needing them to feel the same. To feel deeply and still not demand anything in return. Isn't that love too, just without an audience?

Sometimes, the love that never reaches the other person teaches you the most about yourself. It reveals how much you're willing to give. How much silence you can hold. How tender your heart is, even when it's invisible.

Maybe love is not about being chosen. Maybe it's about what it awakens in you.

So, ask yourself honestly: do you love because you want to be loved back, or do you love because something in you needed to express that feeling, no matter the outcome?

And if there's no response, will you still carry the feeling gently, or will you throw it away like it meant nothing?

Maybe the truest love is the one that doesn't need proof.

Maybe the quietest hearts are the bravest ones.
Maybe love can exist in fragments
Even if no one ever writes you back.
And isn't this what is devotion?
We never ask God to love us back.
We don't wait for Him to say the words first.
Still, we love. We pray. We surrender. We believe.
Even in silence, even without reply...

16

When Love Claims to Have No Conditions

But why then does betrayal still break it?

We love to believe in the nobility of unconditional love.

Love that never fades, no matter the hurt.

Love that keeps giving, even when it receives nothing in return.

Love that says, *"I am here, always."*

But here's the question no one asks:

If love is truly unconditional, then why does betrayal destroy it?

Why does the warmth you once carried in your chest turn into bitterness overnight?

Why does the name that made you smile now make you look away in silence?

We often claim, *"I'll love you no matter what."*

But we don't really mean *no matter what.*

We mean: *as long as you don't lie to me.*

As long as you don't abandon me.

As long as you don't make me feel like I never mattered.

Our love, though deep, comes with invisible conditions.

Unspoken lines we never articulate but feel deeply when they are crossed.

And perhaps, there's no shame in that.

To love is human.

And to be human is to need:

Safety. Honesty. Loyalty.

A certain kind of being seen.

Even a mother, the symbol of unconditional love, sometimes aches to be cared for.

So how can we, fragile as we are, love endlessly when someone breaks us?

You may believe your love is unconditional until the day your trust is fractured.

And then something shifts.

You look at the person you once adored and wonder how you ever let them that close.

The laughter, the promises, the soft touch all now stained by the memory of betrayal.

Does that mean your love was false?

No. It means it was *real.*

And real things bleed when cut.

Unconditional love is a beautiful idea.

But maybe it's not love that has to be unconditional; maybe it's our capacity for empathy, for forgiveness, for letting go.

He told her, "I love you unconditionally."

She smiled, not because she believed it, but because it was a beautiful thing to hear.

He stayed through her mood swings, her distance, her chaos.

He listened to her silences, forgave her delays, and watched her slowly fade into someone he could no longer recognize.

Still, he said he loved her.

No matter what.

But one day, she didn't text for weeks. She stopped checking in.

And something inside him began to ache not from her absence,

but from the quiet expectation that she *should have stayed,*

if only to *deserve* his so-called "unconditional" love.

That's when he saw it clearly.

Even the purest love quietly wants to be seen.

Wants to be felt back.

Wants something even if it claims not to.

"Even unconditional love waits at the door, hoping someone will open it from the other side."

17

The Currency of Attention

Maybe we fall for the feeling, not the person.

We like to say:

"I miss her."

"I miss us."

"I can't move on."

But look closer, and sometimes the ache isn't for the person.

It's for the attention.

The way they looked at you when no one else did.

The way your name felt safe in their mouth.

The way you mattered—to someone.

When a breakup happens, the first pain isn't always about love lost.

It's about silence.

The sudden absence of being seen, noticed, remembered.

The notifications that no longer come.

The "How was your day?" that now belongs to no one.

Have you ever asked yourself:

Did you love them?

Or did you love how you felt when they were around?

We rarely speak this truth.

Because it makes our grief sound shallow.

But it's not shallow—it's *human.*

Love, often, is just the name we give to the emotional attention we receive consistently.

And when it's taken away, our brain searches desperately for the next source.

That's why so many people fall into the arms of someone new, quickly.

Not because they've moved on.

But because they were addicted to the feeling—and they're trying to replicate it, transfer it, fix the withdrawal.

They aren't healing. They're substituting.

They're not falling in love again.

They're falling back into the comfort of being wanted.

Read Receipts

Naina never opened Rohan's messages right away. She'd glance at them when they popped up on her lock screen, her lips curling into a faint smile, and then… she'd put her phone down. She liked knowing he was waiting.

Rohan would check his phone every few minutes, refreshing chats, wondering if she was busy, or worse, losing interest. His mind created a thousand explanations for her delay, all while his heart held on to the tiniest hope that maybe she was just finding the right words to reply.

For Naina, this wasn't about cruelty. It was about control. Each unread message was proof she still mattered to him proof she could summon his thoughts without even being present. It wasn't love. It wasn't even care. It was a subtle addiction to being wanted.

Rohan mistook this hunger for attention as a sign of deep connection, not realizing that sometimes, people don't crave you, they crave the power your attention gives them.

"Some people don't hold your hand; they just hold your mind, so you can't walk away."

18

Love Begins Where Possession Ends

But most of what we call love is just a subtle form of ownership.

What we commonly call love—is it truly love?

Or is it a projection of our loneliness, our craving, our conditioned images of beauty and safety?

Look closely.

The love you feel—does it arise from freedom or from fear?

Do you love the person, or do you love what they make you feel?

And if they stopped making you feel that way would the love remain?

We do not fall in love with another.

We fall into *dependence on what they provide.*

A feeling. A relief. An escape from ourselves.

That's why we say *"I cannot live without you."*

Not because we have touched something eternal,

but because we have become *addicted* to what that person temporarily cures in us.

This is not love. This is need.

Real love begins when you stop needing.

When you are whole and still choose to be with someone without asking them to complete you.

Love is not about being loved back.

It is not about being held, praised, or chosen.

It is about seeing someone *as they are*, without wanting to possess, change, or use them.

But most people don't want this kind of love.

They want comfort.

They want someone to fulfill their script.

That's why relationships break—not because love fades,

but because expectation grows and expectation is violence.

To expect someone to behave a certain way, to remain the same forever,

to always treat us according to our needs—this is not love;

this is psychological imprisonment.

We imprison the other with our desires,

and then complain when they stop being who they once were.

A relationship built on consciousness is very different.

It has no security.

It has no future written in fear.

It is alive in the present moment—vulnerable, honest, free.

But freedom frightens people.

So they choose bondage, and name it love.

Sit with this question:

If the person you love suddenly gave you nothing, no attention, no validation, no presence, would your love remain, or would it rot into resentment?

If it rots, then it was never love.

It was an agreement, a transaction.

The Disguise of Affection

Aarav met Meera during their first year of college. She wasn't the prettiest girl in the room, but she was the only one who remembered his favourite flavour of chips and sent him memes at 2 a.m. They started talking every day, and soon Aarav felt like he'd found "the one".

For him, love became their late-night calls, her checking if he'd eaten, the way she laughed at his dumbest jokes. He didn't realize it, but he was getting addicted, not to her as a person, but to the *attention* she gave him.

Months passed, and whenever Meera took a little longer to reply or seemed less excited, Aarav felt something break inside. He'd scroll back through old chats just to convince himself she still cared. The fear of losing that feeling kept him restless.

One day, Meera told him she needed more space, that she wanted to focus on herself for a while. Aarav didn't feel happy for her—he just felt empty. That's when it hit him: he wasn't in love with *her*. He was in love with the way she made him feel. And when that feeling started to fade, so did his so-called love.

"Sometimes we're not in love with a person; we're in love with our reflection in their eyes."

19

Wanting Love, or Just Wanting to Not Feel Left Out?

Desire is often not yours; it is borrowed from the world around you.

He looks around.

Everyone is in a relationship.

Photos. Stories. Smiles.

Holding hands in the street. Celebrating anniversaries. Texting at midnight.

And so he says, *"I need a girlfriend."*

But stop. Pause. Ask deeply:

Is that a true desire? Or is it just the echo of what he sees around him?

You open Instagram.

There's a couple dancing on a beach, laughing.

Another is having dinner, filming a "cute moment."

Some are travelling, gifting, posting long captions about how lucky they are to have each other.

You scroll past ten stories, and eight of them are of couples.

And somewhere inside you, something stirs.

Not peace. Not joy.

But a quiet sense of lack.

A whisper that says:

"I want this too."

But is it love you're craving?

Or are you simply reacting to what you've been made to believe you *should* have?

We rarely examine the origin of our wants.

We assume because a desire arises within us, it must be ours.

But most desires are injected into us—by society, media, friends, trends, and comparison.

We want what others have, not because it brings us peace,

but because *not having it* makes us feel less than them.

This is how need enters and disguises itself as love.

Next time you see a romantic reel, ask yourself:

"Is this awakening a truth in me, or just reminding me of what I don't have?"

20

Made of Presence, Not Proximity

We stayed far, but the feeling never did.

Have you ever seen two people love each other truly, deeply, but never touch? Never held hands, never hugged, never kissed? I haven't. Not in my surroundings. Not in the world I've known. It almost feels impossible… like something that belongs to a different time, or a different planet.

Because when two people feel that first wave of attraction, something natural, something instinctive begins to happen. The body responds. The mind follows. And often, the distance between them collapses not through thoughts or silence, but through touch.

If the only reason two people are together is because of attraction, then it is almost certain that they will become physical. Very soon. It's as if nature itself has arranged it that way—as if love, when born out of desire, is destined to find its fulfillment in the body.

But then I wonder… is there another kind of love?

A love that isn't ruled by desire, but by understanding. A love that lives in silence, in presence, in memory. One that doesn't ask to be touched, only to be felt.

They say love is complete when no need remains. That when two people are deeply present with each other, even without words, without gestures, without physical contact, there's a kind of closeness that goes beyond the senses.

A communion. A silent merging.

But if no one around me has experienced it, if no one I know has lived it, then is it even real? Or is it just another beautiful lie we tell ourselves when reality fails us?

Yet something inside me doesn't fully accept that. Something resists the idea that love must always become physical. That love, to be real, must pass through the body.

Because I've felt something else. I don't know what to name it. Maybe it wasn't love in the traditional sense. Maybe it was just awareness… or longing… or a connection that refused to ask for more. But it was there.

There was someone I never touched. Never held. Never sat beside. And still, it felt like something moved between us. Quietly. Slowly. Like water moving through roots underground.

Sometimes I think about them and wonder, what if we had met more often, what if the timing had been different, what if we had crossed that invisible line? But then another part of me knows: maybe the beauty of it was in its incompletion. In the fact that nothing happened… and yet everything was felt.

Isn't it strange? That someone can live inside you without ever being close? That a person you never touched could still feel like home for a while?

Some relationships exist outside time. Outside space. Outside need.

And maybe that's the most honest kind of love there is.

The Distance That Didn't Matter

They never met in real life.

Not even once.

Just messages. Late-night calls. Voice notes that felt like whispers.

Two strangers on opposite sides of a screen,

but somehow, closer than anyone who sat beside them every day.

He never touched her hand.

But he held her silence.

She never saw his room.

But she knew what his mind looked like at 3 a.m.

They didn't share coffee.

But they shared fears.

Not meals, but memories.

Not walks, but wounds.

And when she cried, miles away,

he stayed up without her asking.

Not to fix her,

but just to be there. Quiet. Breathing. Present.

People asked, *"But how can it be real if you've never even met?"*

And he smiled.

Because they didn't understand,

love isn't always made of skin.

Sometimes, it's made of soul.

Of attention. Of listening. Of showing up, even from a thousand km away.

It was never about proximity.

It was about presence.

And some presences can be felt across oceans.

21

The Illusion of Always

"Most relationships don't end in forever. They end in learning."

When you enter a relationship, remember this truth: you are not entering a promise, but a possibility.

And possibilities come with odds.

We grow up dreaming of permanence, of the one who'll stay, who'll never leave. But if we look at life honestly, statistically, philosophically, emotionally, most relationships don't last. Not because people lie. Not because love is fake. But because people change. Situations change. The mind moves. And so do hearts.

There's something deeply liberating about walking into a relationship while holding this quiet understanding:

"There is a 99% chance that this will not last forever. But I will still live it fully."

You'll still feel. You'll still care. But you won't break when the goodbye comes, because somewhere inside, you had already made space for it.

Society trains us to chase completion. But what if relationships are not to be completed—only experienced?

Breakups hurt the most when we carry the illusion of permanence. When we fall in love thinking, *"This is it."* But what if you fall in love knowing, *"This may not be it, but it is something."*

Look around. How many teenage relationships become marriages? How many college lovers walk the aisle together? Very few.

Last Seen Today at 2:14 AM

They used to talk every night.

Not call—just messages. Paragraphs. Memes. Spotify links.

A heart react at 1:46 a.m.

A "go sleep now idiot" at 2:00.

It wasn't official. Nothing ever was.

But it felt consistent. Soft. Like they were building something without naming it.

She once said: *"I don't think I'll ever get bored of talking to you."*

He screenshotted it. Saved it in a hidden folder, along with her blurry selfies.

And then slowly, the replies came late.

Then shorter.

Then blue ticks without responses.

The conversation didn't break. It dissolved.

Like a song fading out instead of stopping.

Now, he still opens the chat sometimes.

Scrolls. Smiles. Hurts. Closes.

Wonders if she ever replays the voice notes. If she still has his playlist saved.

She didn't block him. Didn't unfriend him.

But it's been months since she typed anything.

The last message she ever sent just said: *"I'll talk to you in a bit."*

Maybe "always" in this generation doesn't end with a goodbye.

It ends with someone going offline… and staying that way.

Growth, healing.

"You might not end up with the one you love today — and that's okay."

A boy and a girl sit on a park bench. They're holding hands, laughing.

The sun is setting, and the breeze touches their faces gently.

The boy turns to her and says,

"You know, I don't know how long this will last. Maybe a month, maybe years. Maybe we'll marry, maybe we won't. But I just want you to know — I'm okay with that. I'll still love you fully. And when the day comes to say goodbye, I'll thank you for being here at all."

She smiles. That's the moment they both become free from the fear of endings.

What hurts more — the breakup, or the broken expectation

22

The Beauty That Lives in Imagination

"What lives in imagination often feels more beautiful than what lives in reality. Because in imagination, nothing breaks."

There is a harsh truth that remains quietly inside every human experience: what we imagine often feels more beautiful than what we actually live. Our mind, when left untouched by reality, becomes a painter—tender, free, and dangerous. It creates perfection where life can only offer fragments. It completes what remains unfinished. It gives colour to people and moments that, in truth, were ordinary. And that is where the illusion begins.

In imagination, we can control everything. We can make the other person softer. We can make silence meaningful. We can edit the past, rewrite conversations, create futures that may never arrive. And what's more, we can remove everything that would have hurt us in real life. The imagination doesn't argue. It doesn't reject. It doesn't leave.

That's why the memories that never happened sometimes feel stronger than the ones that did. Because they were born entirely within us—shaped and preserved by our own mind. No external force could damage them no other person could distort them. They lived in a pure space. And purity, in this world, is always rare.

Reality, on the other hand, is messy. People forget. Words get misunderstood. Emotions change. Timing is wrong. What once felt magical begins to rust under daily repetition. Expectations grow heavier. Bodies get tired. You cannot imagine someone perfectly forever—not when you have to meet them every day in real form.

That is why we often long not for the person, but for the *idea* we had of them. Not for the relationship, but for the *feeling* that once existed in the mind. That private world where everything was gentle, where nothing ever went wrong.

Imagination is the last safe place. Because it is the only space where things do not break.

The mind is cruel in how it brings us back to these imagined places. But it is also kind. Because when the world forgets to be beautiful, the mind remembers.

The Girl on the Train

He saw her once.

In a crowded train.

Orange scarf. A book in her hand she never opened.

She was not talking. Just breathing, softly, like someone who belonged to silence.

He never spoke to her.

He thought he would.

But something about her presence felt like a dream he didn't want to interrupt.

When she got off at the next station,

he didn't follow.

And yet—for weeks, she lived in his mind.

He gave her a name. A voice. A laugh.

He imagined what she thought about late at night.

He imagined how she might say his name, had she ever known it.

There was no heartbreak. No goodbye.

Only the warmth of something that could have been, but never needed to be.

Sometimes he wondered—

if he had spoken to her, would she still feel so perfect in his memory?

Because in imagination, nothing breaks, nothing fades, and love stays exactly as it was in the first moment—untouched by reality.

23

Where Love Breaks, Friendship Stays

It is because friendship never demanded forever; it simply stayed, without asking to be held.

We often ask: *Why do friendships last, but relationships break?*

They both begin with care. They both share time, laughter, presence.

Yet something in love makes it fragile.

And something in friendship makes it endure.

Why?

Because friendship doesn't ask to possess.

It says: *Be who you are—and I'll still be here.*

But love, especially romantic love, slowly becomes a contract:

Give me what I give you. Don't change. Don't drift. Stay close. Stay mine.

And when one breaks that silent contract, it begins to bleed.

Love often wraps itself in expectations, not always spoken, but deeply felt.

You text less; they feel distant.

You stop calling at night; they wonder if something is wrong.

You choose silence one evening; they think you've changed.

But friendship is more forgiving.

You don't talk for months—yet nothing's lost.

You cancel plans, and no one takes it personally.

You change, and your friend simply updates their understanding of you.

Why this difference?

Because friendship never pretends to own you.

It exists in freedom, while love often demands exclusivity.

In the Quiet Space Between Us

Two people sat on a terrace.

One had once loved the other. Deeply. Loudly. Painfully.

Now, they laughed about a meme. Shared their work stress.

No tension. No invisible expectation.

The one who once loved thought:

Strange. When I wanted more, we broke.

Now that I want nothing, we sit here, whole.

A relationship often wants intensity.

Friendship settles for consistency.

Love asks: *Do you still feel the same?*

Friendship says: *I'm still here, even if we've changed.*

Maybe that's why lovers become strangers, but old friends remain

a text away, a call away, and sometimes, just a memory away from comfort.

"The heart may forget the name it once whispered in the dark, but it remembers the hands that held us in silence."

24

When You Didn't Know Me, You Loved Me More

"We were better as a feeling than we ever were as people."

There was a time you didn't know me.

And maybe, back then, you loved me more.

I've realized something strange.

When people look back after a breakup, they rarely smile thinking about their ex.

But somehow, they still smile when they remember their *crush.*

Not the one they dated.

The one they *imagined* dating.

That's the difference.

A crush is untouched by truth.

It exists in distance, in silence, in hope, not in reality.

And because it was never touched, it never had the chance to break.

The moment you came closer, things changed.

The way you looked at me became different.

The way I tried to hold on, the way you slowly slipped, all of it became heavy.

I've started believing:

You didn't fall out of love.

You just saw me too closely.

And maybe that's the tragedy.

We were perfect only in distance.

Maybe closeness ruined what the distance had kept safe.

From far, everything looks beautiful.

Like a city from a hilltop. Or stars in the sky.

But when you go close, you see the noise, the cracks, the silence inside the lights.

That's what love becomes when it replaces longing.

It becomes reality. And reality has no filter.

I don't blame you.

I don't even blame myself.

We both loved the *idea* of each other.

Not the person behind it.

And in the end, when everything faded, it wasn't the relationship I missed;

It was the version of you I had created in my head before you ever spoke to me.

That version never hurt me.

That version never changed.

That version never left.

I saw her again after years.

Not my ex, my old school crush.

She was just standing at a signal, scrolling through her phone like nothing had changed.

And in that moment, something in me smiled.

Not because I still loved her.

Not because I wanted her back.

But because she never hurt me.

She never said anything that broke me. She was never mine. And maybe that's why the memory of her still feels peaceful.

25

The Ledger of Love

"The heart keeps no records, until it is left alone."

There is a strange thing that happens when love ends. During the relationship, the giving feels natural, almost invisible. You buy them their favourite coffee, listen to them on nights they are breaking down, walk miles just to see them smile. None of it feels like an effort at the time; it feels like breathing.

But when the bond breaks, something shifts. The same actions that once felt effortless begin to weigh on you like stones. You start counting, not money, not hours, but efforts. "I was there when no one else was." "I gave them my time, my patience, my care." And in this quiet accounting, there is both pain and pride.

Why do we do this? Perhaps it is because, when love is gone, we are left holding receipts for emotions we can no longer spend. We go back and tally the nights we stayed awake for them, the days we sacrificed our comfort, the dreams we postponed just to see theirs bloom. And in remembering, we cry, not just because they are gone, but because all that giving now has nowhere to go.

Some say it is regret; I think it is a search for meaning. We want to believe that our efforts mattered, that they left an imprint on the other person's life. And maybe they did. Maybe they still carry the warmth of our presence even if they no longer stand beside us.

Love, when alive, is free of calculation. It does not measure. But when it dies, the human mind turns into an auditor, examining every little act as if to answer the question: "Was it worth it?" And maybe the answer is never clear, because the value of love was never in its balance sheet—it was in the moments we lived without counting at all.

It is strange how, after separation, memory changes its shape.

We stop replaying the laughter, the gentle glances, the shared silences.

Instead, we start playing a cruel accounting game:

"I did this much for you. I gave you that. I stayed up late for you. I travelled miles for you."

Every act of love suddenly wears the costume of a burden, as if it was dragged out of us instead of given freely.

But in reality, no one forced us.

They didn't hand us a checklist, saying,

"Here's what you must do if you want my love."

We made those choices because, in that moment, loving them felt like the most natural thing in the world.

The late-night calls, the surprise gifts, the skipped meals, the sacrifices, all of them were things we *wanted* to do.

So why, when it's over, do we act like we were victims of our own generosity?

Maybe it's not the loss of the person that hurts the most

it's the sudden feeling that all our efforts had no lasting meaning.

We want our love to matter, even after it's gone.

We want the other person to carry our efforts like precious treasures, not discard them like yesterday's flowers.

"A Lesson from the Garden"

A student came to one of the sisters, upset and confused.

"Sister, I did so much for him—helped him with his studies, stayed up late when he was sick, even gave him my favourite book. But now he's left, and I feel empty and hurt. Why does it feel like all I did was for nothing?"

The sister smiled kindly and asked,

"When you water the plants in the school garden, do you expect the flowers to thank you or give you something back?"

The student thought for a moment and said,

"No, I water them because I want them to grow and bloom."

The sister said, *"Exactly. Love is like that watering. If you gave your care and effort without being asked, then you gave from your own heart. Why then do you keep counting your giving now, as if you expect something in return? True love never keeps score—it simply flows."*

The student sat quietly, realizing that love given freely is its own reward, and that pain often comes when we start thinking love is a transaction.

26

The Glow That Comes After Goodbye

Maybe it takes a goodbye to remind us who we really are to reignite the quiet light within.

It's strange, isn't it? How after a breakup, people suddenly start to bloom. There's the gym routine, the new wardrobe, the confidence that begins to return, the spark that says, *"I'm coming back to myself."*

But why does this awakening, wait until love ends? Why do we wait for pain to push us toward becoming?

Because a breakup is not just an ending; it's a shock that jolts the soul awake. It tears away the layers we hid beneath, the parts that grew silent in the comfort of routine. It's a kind of unmasking: brutal, honest, but necessary. The fears surface, the wounds ache, and yet, beneath it all, something sacred stirs strength.

The glow-up isn't vanity. It's resurrection. It's the stepping out from the shadows it once agreed to live in. The long walks, the late-night journaling, the rediscovery of music or art—they are not distractions. They are small rebellions against what once confined us. They are whispers of *"I am still here."*

When we're in love, we often trade small parts of ourselves for the comfort of togetherness. We stop chasing the things that make us come alive because we start chasing someone else. And when love leaves, the silence that follows becomes an invitation a space to meet ourselves again.

Maybe that's the hidden gift inside heartbreak: it demands growth. It forces a kind of reckoning that comfort never could. The pain burns, yes, but it also purifies. It teaches us to shine not to be seen, but to remember that we exist, fully, fiercely, and enough on our own.

"The Beginning After Goodbye"

Maya and Aarav shared three years of laughter and silence, dreams whispered and forgotten.

In love, Maya folded her colours away, hiding her brushes beneath layers of 'compromise.'

Her mornings lost to sleep, her spark dimmed in quiet surrender.

Then came the day the door closed, softly, yet with the weight of a storm.

In that silence, Maya heard a whisper, a call to remember herself.

She woke before dawn, breathed in the cool air, and let her fingers dance across empty canvases.

Clothes once hidden now embraced her skin like a new song.

She moved to rhythms she'd forgotten, wrote words her heart had longed to speak.

A friend asked, "Why did this glow come only after the goodbye?"

Smiling, with tears shining like the dawn, Maya said, "Sometimes, to find yourself, you first have to lose what you thought was love.

The end was not a death, but a beginning, a rebirth into the light I forgot I carried all along."

27

Nothing Was Mine, Everything Was Felt

Not every story needs a belonging. Some are just meant to pass through you and they change you.

We didn't date.

We weren't "a thing."

We had no status, no photos, no label.

But we had presence.

The kind that sits with you during lunch breaks, not because they have to, but because they *want to.*

The kind that sends a song at 1 a.m. with no message, yet says everything.

The kind that remembers your viva date, your chai preference, your anxiety patterns.

It wasn't anything, and yet somehow, it was everything.

I never had her.

Not officially. Not emotionally. Not really.

But in moments, she was there.

And presence, even when brief, is more honest than promises that collapse under the weight of time.

Love, we're taught, is something to secure.

To post. To name. To make "official."

But what if the truest form of love is not what's held

but what's simply *witnessed*, deeply and clearly, for a while?

It's strange, how someone can still feel close

when the only trace of them now is an Instagram story you view in silence.

No likes. No replies. Just passive proof that they're still breathing.

We become digital ghosts in each other's lives, there, but untouchable.

Online, but never really… with us.

And yet, one seen story can ruin your day.

That's how memory plays tricks:

not in what it shows, but in what it *withholds.*

What if it's not about owning the person but experiencing the feeling?

We want our stories to fit categories:

Friend. Lover. Ex. Crush.

But sometimes, people don't fit boxes.

They just exist, like a question you never found the answer to.

A poem half-remembered.

A truth half-swallowed.

And maybe that's okay.

Maybe love, like rain, is not meant to be collected, only felt when it falls.

She was never mine.

We didn't make memories to post.

We didn't promise forever.

We didn't end with closure.

But I remember how my voice softened when I said her name.

I remember how her silence taught me more than her presence.

Nothing was mine.

Everything was felt.

And maybe that was enough.

28

If You Ever Read This

If you ever read this, I want you to know that nothing I wrote was ever really about "love" in some abstract sense; it was always about you. Every sentence, every quiet metaphor, every question I threw at the sky was just my way of speaking to you without saying your name.

I wonder if you will recognise yourself here. In the pages where I wrote about the way love fades but memories remain, that was you. In the parts where I spoke about the ache of wanting to stay but knowing you had to leave, that was you. Even when I pretended to be wise, as if I had understood the nature of love, I was just a boy trying to understand the nature of losing you.

I wonder if you will feel the pauses between my words, those moments where I stopped writing because I suddenly remembered something small: the way your hair fell when you laughed, the way you looked away when you were trying not to smile. I never wrote those details down, but they lived in my head, unshakable, like an old song you can't forget even after years.

And maybe you won't recognise yourself at all. Maybe you'll think I'm writing about someone else. Maybe you'll forget that I ever noticed how you always ordered two spoons for dessert, even when you were eating alone, just in case. But I'll know. And that's enough.

I'm not writing this to make you come back. I'm not writing this to change your mind. I'm writing this because it feels wrong for a story like ours to disappear without leaving some kind of footprint. If I can't have you in my life, at least I can have you in my pages.

If you ever read this, I hope it doesn't hurt you. I hope it makes you smile. I hope you see that in this world where people keep searching for the perfect love, I was just grateful to have had something real, even if it didn't last forever.

"Some people leave, but they never really go; they just live between your words, waiting to be read again."

Closing Note to the Reader

If you reached here—

thank you for carrying these fragments with me.

This wasn't just a book.

It was a quiet sitting with memory,

a hand extended toward everything we feel but never say.

Maybe you found your own reflections between these pages,

a sentence that resembled your past,

a wound that looked like yours,

a goodbye you still carry quietly in your heart.

If so,

I hope this didn't heal you.

I hope it reminded you that you didn't need to be healed in the first place.

That feeling deeply even the ache is proof that you lived honestly.

In a world chasing forever,

thank you for finding beauty in the fleeting.

—*Naman Goswami*

About the Author

Naman Goswami doesn't write to impress. He writes to awaken.

In a time when love is either worshipped blindly or dismissed without thought, he chooses to stand still and watch. This book isn't meant to teach what love is. It only asks you to notice it—how it shapes the mind, how it moves through the body, how memory and longing quietly build our sense of closeness.

No one really wants to slow down with love anymore. Everyone wants quick answers, perfect stories, or clean endings.

Few want to look at love with open eyes without illusion, without fear, without escaping.

This book is a small act against that silence. It tries to hold love softly, to look at it honestly, and to ask one simple question:

What truly happens inside us when we say, "I love you"?